THE
Baffling
Baseball
MYSTERY

First Edition ©2012 Carole Marsh/Gallopade International/Peachtree City, GA
Current Edition ©February 2014
Ebook edition ©2013
All rights reserved.
Manufactured in Peachtree City, GA

Carole Marsh Mysteries™ and its skull colophon are the property of Carole Marsh and
Gallopade International.

Published by Gallopade International/Carole Marsh Books. Printed in the United States
of America.

Editor: Janice Baker
Assistant Editor: Sherri Smith Brown
Cover Design: Vicki DeJoy
Content Design: Randolyn Friedlander

Gallopade International is introducing SAT words that kids need to know in each
new book that we publish. The SAT words are bold in the story. Look for each
word in the special SAT glossary. Happy Learning!!

Gallopade is proud to be a member and supporter of these educational organizations
and associations:

American Booksellers Association
American Library Association
International Reading Association
National Association for Gifted Children
The National School Supply and Equipment Association
The National Council for the Social Studies
Museum Store Association
Association of Partners for Public Lands
Association of Booksellers for Children
Association for the Study of African American Life and History
National Alliance of Black School Educators

Once upon a time...

Hmm, kids keep asking me to write a mystery book. What shall I do?

Mimi

Write one about spiders!

You two really are characters, that's all I've got to say!

Yes you are! And, of course I choose you! But what should I write about?

National Parks!

SCARY PLACES!

FAMOUS PLACES!

FUN PLACES!

Disney World!

 New York City!

Dracula's Castle

 **GRAND CANYON**

On the *Mystery Girl* airplane ...

I can FLY US anyWHeRe!

Mystery Girl

Or aboard the *Mimi!*

Mimi

Take me to the Forbidden City!

Or by surfboard, rickshaw, motorbike, camel ...

All great ideas! I can put a lot of history, **MYSTERY,** legend, lore, and **laughs** in the books! We can use other boys and girls in the books. It will be educational and fun!

Good stuff!

And so, Mimi, Papa, Christina, and Grant took off aboard the *Mystery Girl* and America's National Mystery Book Series—where the adventure is real and so are the characters! —was born.

START YOUR ADVENTURE TODAY!

READ THE BOOK!

GO ONLINE!

TRACK YOUR ADVENTURES!

APPLY TO BE A CHARACTER!

Yikes! That was close!

Rats!

1
BATTER UP!

"Let's go, teeeam! Let's go!"

Grant could hear the chants of his teammates from the dugout. He was in his shortstop ready position: open stance, knees slightly bent, and poised to move left or right at any time. His glove was open toward the batter. He was set to catch anything that came his way. His blue eyes stared intently at the batter.

It was a hot, steamy August night in Atlanta, Georgia. Grant's youth baseball team had won their summer league championship game last week. Now, they were playing a demonstration game at Turner Field right before an Atlanta Braves home baseball game. The kids were only playing two innings, but Grant was excited!

The crowds slowly drifted into their seats. Braves players were appearing in the dugout. Grant caught a glimpse of his hero, Braves third baseman Chipper Jones.

"Hit that ball!" he said under his breath. "Hit that ball! Hit that ball! And if you do, I'll catch it!"

It was the top of the second inning. Grant's team was behind, 2 – 1, with two outs.

Grant's teammate Roberto Sanchez wound up and pitched a blazing fastball. The batter swung. "Strike!" yelled the umpire.

That's strike one, thought Grant. *Fire another one in there, Roberto!*

"Yea! Roberto!" chanted the kids in the dugout. "Do it again! Do it again!!"

Roberto hurled another fastball, a little low and inside. But the batter golfed it up—a little blooper coming right at Grant!

He lunged toward the ball. It bounced in front of him but Grant scooped it up. *That was a close one!* he thought, as he spun around and shot the ball to the first baseman.

THUD! Grant's feet came out from under him. Dirt flew as his bottom hit the ground. But the first baseman made a solid catch just ahead of the runner.

"OUT!" yelled the first base umpire, clenching his fist and making a hammer motion. The crowd cheered! The inning was over!

Grant jumped up and sprinted toward the dugout, pumping his fist. *I wonder if Chipper saw me*, he thought, looking for his idol.

Christina yawned and stretched. She was watching her brother play ball from the stands right behind his dugout. Roberto's sister Jennifer sat beside Christina. She was clapping wildly.

"Yeaaaa!" yelled Jennifer. "Way to go after that ball, Grant!" She picked up her scorebook and pencil and marked the out. "Now, let's get some runs, you guys!" she cheered. Jennifer's wavy brown ponytail stuck out through the loop in her light blue ball cap. It swung back and forth as she danced around in her seat.

"Great play!" shouted Christina and Grant's grandmother Mimi. Her ruby red bangle bracelets jingled as she jumped up and down and clapped.

Papa, the kids' grandfather, waved his black cowboy hat at Grant. Christina gave Grant two thumbs up. A wide grin spread across Grant's face when he saw them cheering in the stands.

Christina wished she enjoyed baseball as much as her grandparents and Jennifer did. But the fact was, she thought baseball was boring. She would much rather be traveling with Mimi and Papa.

Mimi was Carole Marsh, the famous children's mystery book writer. Papa flew his little airplane, the *Mystery Girl*, all over the country while Mimi researched her books. Lots of times, Christina and Grant got to go along. In fact, they were leaving first thing in the morning for a baseball road trip. Mimi was going to research old baseball players and games for a new book. Jennifer and Roberto were going with them.

But why does it have to be about baseball? thought Christina. She pushed her straight, medium-length brown hair behind her ears.

Christina enjoyed being at Turner Field, though. She liked the way Atlanta's skyline twinkled behind the stadium's left-field wall as the sun started to sink. The massive Coca-Cola bottle stood tall against the sky. The blue Delta Air Lines sign with its red logo glowed in the outfield. A huge video screen played clips of exciting catches and hits. She liked the music, the popcorn, and the peanuts. The fireworks were fun too! She just didn't like baseball.

She plucked a pair of dark sunglasses from her backpack. *Maybe no one will notice if I sleep*, she thought.

A man sitting in front of Jennifer turned around and looked at Mimi and Papa. "Are you related to that shortstop out there?" he asked.

"He's our grandson," said Papa proudly. "His team won their championship last week."

"He's a good little shortstop," said the man. "My name's Slugger McCoy," he added, reaching back to shake Papa's hand. Slugger McCoy wore a tattered Braves ball cap. His Braves t-shirt was frayed around the sleeves. He, too, had an open scorebook on his lap and a pencil behind his ear.

Soon the two men were immersed in a baseball conversation. Slugger had played on a minor league baseball team when he was young. He had dreamed about going to the "Big Show," but it had never happened for him.

"What's the 'Big Show'?" asked Christina.

"This," said Slugger, extending his left arm in a sweeping gesture around the field. "Major league baseball. The stadium! The crowds! The cheers! Do you like baseball?" he asked Christina.

"Not so much," said Christina. "Girls don't have much opportunity to play baseball, so I'm not that interested in it."

"You could play softball like I do," said Jennifer. She wore a light blue and white t-shirt with "Peaches" displayed across the front and her name and number 15 on the back.

"Softball sounds like fun," said Christina politely. "But it seems even slower than baseball to me."

WHACK! Just then, Roberto hit a ground ball to left field and raced to first base.

"Wooo hooo, Roberto!" shouted Jennifer. "Way to go, brother!"

"Baseball is a great game," said Slugger. "And you don't have to play it to love it!"

"Do you miss playing?" asked Christina.

"Sure," said Slugger. "If I couldn't watch it, I would be miserable." He chuckled. "No, you surely don't have to play baseball to appreciate it. It has such a colorful and interesting history. It's the 'All American' game! Did you know baseball is often compared to life?"

"That it is!" said Mimi, shaking her blond head up and down.

Christina scrunched up her eyebrows. "What do you mean?" she asked.

Slugger laughed. "If you do something good," he said, "you 'hit a homerun' or 'you knock it out of the park'!"

"You 'step up to the plate' when you take responsibility for something," said Papa.

"And people always want to come 'home'!" added Mimi.

"Hey, look, Grant's up to bat!" said Papa.

Grant's blond curls crept out from under his dark blue batter's helmet. He eyed the situation as he slowly walked up to the batter's box. There were two outs. Roberto stood on second base. Grant needed to hit the ball hard enough to get Roberto home so they would win.

"Bring him in! Bring him in!" Grant's team screamed from the dugout.

Grant took a couple of practice swings and stepped up to the plate. He settled into his stance and focused on the pitcher. The pitcher threw a low fastball. Grant swung. "Strike!" called the ump.

Grant backed away from the plate a little. Then he approached again. He planted his feet. His bat tottered over his right shoulder. The pitcher wound up and threw the ball. Grant's eyes were glued to the white sphere coming right at him.

WHACK!

He made contact. The ball sailed over the head of the right fielder and rolled toward the back wall. Grant ran for his life, squarely hitting the bases as he rounded the diamond. Roberto tagged home plate with Grant on his heels. Two runs scored on an in-the-park home run! The crowd roared! Jennifer jumped up and down. Papa hugged Mimi while Christina leaped up and clapped for her brother.

Christina noticed that Slugger McCoy had a big smile on his face. "Great game!" he said to her. "Great game!"

2
BEANEATERS, BATS, AND BALLS!

Grant and Roberto gawked at the Braves' 1995 World Series trophy. The two-foot tall trophy gleamed. It was enclosed in a four-sided glass case in the Braves Museum and Hall of Fame. Thirty tiny, gold plated flags on thin spindles rose from the base of the trophy. There was one flag for each major league team.

"Now that's a trophy!" exclaimed Grant. "Look, it says, 'World Series Champions Atlanta Braves.' Yeah!"

"The Braves won fourteen straight National League Division Championships," said Jennifer, "from 1991 to 2005."

"How did you know that?" asked Grant.

"She's good at remembering statistics," said Roberto proudly. "Statistics, or 'stats' for short, are numbers about baseball!" His brown eyes twinkled. "Our mom and dad are good, too. We quiz each other at dinnertime. They especially loved Roberto Clemente!"

"Aha!" exclaimed Papa. "The famous right fielder for the Pittsburgh Pirates! Were you named for him?"

"I sure was!" said Roberto. "He was born in Puerto Rico like my parents. They say he helped a lot of poor people in Puerto Rico. He used to bring them food and baseball equipment."

"He played with the Pirates from 1955 to 1972," said Jennifer. "He was the National League's Most Valuable Player in 1966. He led the league in batting average for four different seasons. He also won twelve Gold Glove Awards. That's an award coaches and managers in each league present every year for superior fielding."

"That's what I want to win someday!" said Grant. He quickly crouched to his shortstop ready position, gobbling up an imaginary ball with an imaginary baseball glove.

"Our parents said he died in an airplane accident," added Roberto. "He was on his way to help people who were in an earthquake."

"Well, your parents certainly honored his memory by naming you after him," said Mimi.

Roberto beamed as the group walked over to another exhibit.

"Did you know the Braves used to play in Boston?" asked Mimi.

"Chipper played for the Boston Red Sox?" said Grant incredulously.

"No," said Mimi, reading the exhibit. "The Braves played there from 1871 to 1952! Long before Chipper was born!"

"Look," said Christina. "It says the Boston Braves were once called the Beaneaters!"

"I'm glad the Braves aren't called the Beaneaters anymore," said Grant. " That sure would be a funny name to have on the back of your jersey!" He pretended to gobble up beans with a spoon.

"Wow!" said Jennifer. "I didn't know Babe Ruth played for the Braves."

"Yep," said Papa. "He played for the Boston Braves in 1935."

"Babe Ruth, the candy bar, played for the Braves?" asked Grant. "I'll bet his uniform was a mess! He probably had chocolate melted all over it!" He and Roberto started to giggle.

"No," said Mimi. "That's a **misnomer** for a lot of people. Baby Ruth is the candy bar. Babe Ruth is the baseball player. He mostly played for Boston and New York. He was a real rough and tumble kind of guy. But he is considered one of the greatest baseball players ever."

"I remember when Hank Aaron hit his 715th home run to beat 'the Babe's' homerun record," said Papa.

"Did you see it?" asked Christina.

"Yes, I did!" said Papa. "It was very exciting. That was back in 1974. The Braves were playing at the old Atlanta Fulton County Stadium. I was right there in the stands. So—one Brave broke another Brave's record! Hey, there's the bat and ball Aaron used when he did it."

The kids ran to the glass case where Hank Aaron's bat and ball were displayed. A yellow tape surrounded the glass case, keeping visitors at a distance. "Why is it blocked off?" Christina asked a museum guide standing nearby.

"Someone tried to steal Hank's bat and ball earlier today," said the guide. "The police are still investigating."

"Why would someone try to steal it?" asked Christina.

"Probably to sell for lots of money," said Papa.

"A lot of people collect baseball memorabilia," added Mimi. "Unfortunately, some dishonest people will put a fake signature on a baseball and sell it to an unsuspecting person. Others steal authentic baseball souvenirs and sell them on the black market."

"What's the black market?" asked Grant. "Is that some kind of dark grocery store? Who wants to shop in a place like that?!"

"Basically," explained Mimi, "the black market refers to the sale of illegal goods or services. If someone stole Hank's bat and ball and sold it to an unethical collector, you would say he sold it on the black market."

Christina shuddered. She had never thought about thieves and black markets for baseball souvenirs. *Why would anyone want to collect that stuff?* she thought.

3
BASEBALL CARDS AND STRANGERS

The kids, Mimi, and Papa walked through the Plaza at Turner Field. Turner Field was originally built for the 1996 Olympics in Atlanta. After the Olympics, it was converted into a stadium for the Braves. There were tons of things to see and do inside and just outside the stadium.

"This place is GREAT!" said Grant. "You don't even have to watch a baseball game to have fun!" He stuffed the last bite of a sloppy chili dog into his mouth.

"There's Homer, the Braves' mascot!" shouted Roberto. The kids swarmed around Homer as Mimi took a photo.

At Tooner Field, the kids played interactive games with their favorite Cartoon Network characters. In Scouts Alley, Jennifer blistered ball after ball to win the home run derby. Roberto fired blazing fastballs to test his pitching speed. And Grant held his own in the batting cage, slamming curve balls into the net. At Sky Field at the top of the stadium, the four sweaty kids raced around the bases.

"Boy, I sure need this!" cried Grant. He spread his arms out wide and let the cool spray of the mist machine cover his face and drip off the tip of his nose.

"Whew! I'm beat," said Mimi. She fanned her face with a game program. "Just watching you has worn me out!"

Papa looked up at one of the television monitors hanging from the ceiling. "It's almost time for the game to start," he said.

"We need to go down to the locker room and get our gear," said Grant.

"Christina, will you go with the boys?" asked Mimi. "Papa and I will get plenty of popcorn and head for the seats."

"I'll go, too," said Jennifer. "Maybe I can get an autograph before the game starts!"

Christina, Grant, Roberto, and Jennifer walked to the tunnel that led to the locker rooms. The crowd was thinning out as fans made their way to their seats.

"You guys go on," said Christina to the boys. "I'll hang out and wait on you."

Grant and Roberto raced into the tunnel.

"I'm going up to the stands to get closer to the dugout," said Jennifer. "Maybe I'll have a better chance of getting a player's attention there."

Christina shoved her hands into her shorts pockets. She walked along, head down, through the dimly lit tunnel. *Maybe I should have tried for an autograph with Jennifer*, she thought.

Suddenly, she spied a baseball card on the ground. Christina stooped down to pick it up.

The card looked old and worn.

"Cool, it's Babe Ruth!" Christina said to herself. She thought about how they had just talked about him earlier today. *Mimi said he was one of the greatest baseball players ever,* she thought. *Someone must have lost this. Maybe it's a sign of good luck since we're going on a baseball road trip tomorrow.*

Christina carefully placed the card deep into her pocket.

Behind her at the far end of the shadowy tunnel, a man watched her. He began moving quickly in her direction.

WHAM! The boys burst through the locker room doors.

"I can't wait to go to Cooperstown tomorrow!" said Roberto. "It's going to be so much fun."

"Don't you think so, Christina?" asked Grant. "It will be baseball, baseball, baseball!"

Christina laughed. "I'll find something to do to have fun," she said. "You know me," she added with a touch of sarcasm, "I'm all about baseball!"

Just then, Slugger McCoy stepped out of the bright light of the stadium and into the dimly lit tunnel. She waved, but he didn't see her.

A security guard walked out of the locker room. He began striding up the tunnel alongside the kids and toward the approaching stranger. "Did you boys get all your things?" the guard asked.

Christina looked up. She saw the stranger. He wore a ball cap pulled down over his eyes. A lumpy black gym bag hung on a strap from his shoulder. He abruptly stopped and hurried away from them. He glanced back once at Christina. Then, he disappeared around the corner of the tunnel.

He sure is weird, Christina thought. *He looked like he was about to tackle us. But why?*

4

RUNNING THE BASES

"Braves win! Braves win!" shouted Grant as he jumped up and down. "Now, let's go run the bases!"

Running the bases is a tradition for kids after Sunday afternoon games at Turner Field. Grant, Roberto, and Jennifer started climbing over the bleachers to get to the field.

"Come on, Christina!" Jennifer yelled.

That's for little kids, Christina thought. "You guys go ahead," she said.

Grant turned toward her. "Come on, Christina! Come on, Christina," he sang. Roberto and Jennifer joined in the chant.

"Oh, OK," Christina mumbled.

"I'll take some pictures," Mimi said, getting out her camera.

Christina moaned. She followed Grant, Roberto, and Jennifer down to the field and got in line. Within a few minutes, she was trotting after them around the diamond.

For some reason, Christina thought about the Babe Ruth baseball card. She gingerly placed her hand inside her pocket and touched the frayed edge of it.

As she ran toward first base, she looked up at the stands. *I wonder what it's like to see thousands of people in the stands cheering for you, she thought. It's too bad girls can't play ball in the major leagues. It must be exciting!*

Ahead of her, Grant crossed home plate. Then Roberto. Then Jennifer. Then it was Christina's turn. She stepped squarely on home plate. She laughed as the other kids gave her a high-five!

"That was fun!" said Jennifer. "I wish I could do it again! Look, there's Slugger McCoy." She pointed to the stands.

Slugger sat in the stands. A shaggy-haired man was talking to him. Christina waved but he seemed to look past her. She thought he looked dejected.

"I guess he doesn't see us," Christina said to Jennifer.

"Who's Slugger McCoy?" asked Grant.

"He sat in front of us while you and Roberto were playing," said Christina. "He used to play baseball."

"He always wanted to play in the Big Show," explained Jennifer. "But he never made it."

Something about Slugger McCoy made Christina feel sad. She wished he would look at her so she could wave.

As the kids came off the field, they passed close by the man with the black gym bag sitting in the stands. Christina saw him pull his ball cap down over his eyes. He seemed to peer at her from under it.

"Why's that guy staring at us?" whispered Grant as they walked up the ramp to a waving Mimi and Papa.

"I don't know," said Christina. "I saw him earlier in the tunnel. He sure is creepy!"

5

I'LL TRADE YOU A DEREK JETER FOR A ROY HALLADAY

Papa's little red and white airplane, the *Mystery Girl*, soared through the hazy summer sky. They were on their way to the National Baseball Hall of Fame and Museum in Cooperstown, New York.

Christina turned off the portable DVD player. The kids had just watched *The Bad News Bears*, a movie about a group of misfit little league players.

"That coach wasn't like any coach I've ever had!" said Grant.

"Only in the movies!" said Christina.

"That girl was a really good pitcher," said Jennifer. "Makes me want to get out and play!"

"You got any new baseball cards?" Roberto asked Grant.

"I bought a couple of packs yesterday," replied Grant. He reached for his black backpack.

"Why do you collect baseball cards?" asked Christina.

Roberto and Grant looked at each other and shook their heads. "Wow, Christina!" said Grant. "I can't believe you said that. EVERYBODY collects baseball cards."

"I just asked WHY," said Christina, pouting a little.

"So we can have a card about our favorite players," said Roberto. "I have a card for Roy Halladay for each season he's played. He's been pitching since 1998."

"It's really fun to trade them, too," Grant added.

"I have baseball cards, too," said Jennifer, her brown eyes twinkling. "That's one of the ways I learn all the players' statistics. I mainly collect the Puerto Rican players."

Grant ripped open one of his new packs of twelve cards. "I've already got this Derek Jeter card," he said. "Anybody want to trade?"

"Derek Jeter," said Jennifer. "Shortstop, throws right, bats right, New York Yankees since 1995."

Grant's mouth flew open. "How do you know all that?" he asked.

"I'm telling you, she's good at that kind of stuff," said Roberto. "I think she has numbers swimming around in her brain!" Grant giggled at the thought.

Jennifer and Roberto dove into their backpacks to pull out their baseball cards. Soon, the kids were looking through each other's cards and quoting statistics about their favorite players.

"Actually, I do have a baseball card!" said Christina quietly.

"You do?" Grant asked, looking up sharply from his pile of cards.

"Who is it?" asked Jennifer.

"I found it at Turner Field yesterday," said Christina, "when you guys were in the locker room." She unzipped the front pocket of her blue and green backpack and pulled out the Babe Ruth card.

"Hmmm," said Grant. "It's kind of old. Who is it?"

"It's Babe Ruth," said Christina. "See, R-U-T-H."

"It doesn't have any stats on it," said Jennifer, surveying the card closely.

"I think I like the newer players better," said Grant.

"Open up your other pack," Roberto said to Grant.

"Do you want some of our extra ones, Christina?" asked Jennifer. "Then you can start collecting."

Christina looked at Babe's photo. "I like this one," she said, sliding it in her jacket pocket. "It's enough for now."

"You kids talking about baseball cards?" called Papa from the pilot's seat. "I used to have a pretty good collection. I sold some of them a couple of years ago."

"I remember that," said Mimi, closing the book she was reading. "That fellow you sold them to was a real character."

"Yep!" said Papa. "His name was Jack LaForge. You should have seen his house—just filled with baseball memorabilia! He had stuff in glass cases and sitting in stacks on the floor. He bought some old Yankees cards from me."

"He BOUGHT your baseball cards?" said Grant. "Did he pay you a million bucks?"

"No!" said Papa. "But they were really good cards. My uncle gave them to me when I was a boy. They represented the five players who made up the 1927 lineup of the New York Yankees. They were nicknamed 'Murderer's Row.' One of them was one of the most famous baseball players of all time—Babe Ruth."

Christina's ears perked up. *Babe Ruth—again*, she thought.

"Look, we're here!" said Papa. "You can see the Adirondack Mountains in the distance. Right down there is Cooperstown."

"It's so beautiful up here!" said Mimi, putting on her red rhinestone sunglasses.

"That must be Otsego Lake. Cooperstown sits on the southern tip of the lake. I bet it's cooler up here than it was in Atlanta!"

Papa tipped the wings of the *Mystery Girl* so everyone could see the mountains, the glimmering blue lake, and the village of Cooperstown.

"Why did they put the Baseball Hall of Fame all the way up here?" asked Grant. "They don't even have a major league baseball team."

"Well, legend has it that the game of baseball was invented in Cooperstown," said Mimi. "We'll learn more about it at the museum."

"I can't wait!" said Jennifer. She smiled as she put on her New York Yankees ball cap.

"Prepare for landing in Cooperstown," said Papa in his best captain's voice. Soon, the *Mystery Girl* was sitting on the airport tarmac, and Papa, Mimi, and the kids were walking into the airport.

Christina took her Babe Ruth baseball card out of her pocket. *No one was even impressed with it,* she thought. She looked at it carefully. *I don't need this old thing.* She started to crumple it up and throw it in a nearby trash can. But something stopped her. She looked at it again. Babe Ruth stared back at her.

Christina felt a shiver run down her spine. She unzipped the front pocket of her backpack. "OK, Babe," she said, putting the card inside. "I'll keep you a little while longer."

44

6
ABNER DOUBLEDAY'S GREAT MYTH

"Here we go!" announced Papa as they walked up to the National Baseball Hall of Fame and Museum. "We've made the pilgrimage to Cooperstown. They say this is the best place to come to honor the game of baseball!"

"It reminds me of an old schoolhouse," said Christina as they entered the three-story brick building.

"It was built in 1939 during the Great Depression," said Mimi. "They were trying to bring tourists to Cooperstown. Today, hundreds of thousands of people come each year."

"So did they invent baseball here?" asked Grant.

"No," said Mimi. "It seems that's just a myth, or a good story."

"What's the story?" asked Roberto.

"This says baseball probably came from a number of different folk games that people played years ago," said Mimi, looking at an exhibit. "The games were played with a bat and ball. One team pitched the ball. The other team hit it and ran bases while the other team tried to get them out by some means."

"What's a fork game?" asked Grant. "Do you play it with a fork?"

"The word is f-o-l-k," said Mimi. "Folk games are games that people make up. There are no rules written down. People play them the way they want to play them."

"What about this man named Abner Doubleday?" asked Jennifer as she read some writing on a nearby exhibit.

"My history teacher said Abner Doubleday was a Union soldier in the Civil War," said Christina. "Somehow, people got the idea that he invented baseball in 1839 in Cooperstown. But he never said he did, and no one is even certain he ever came to Cooperstown."

"That's very strange," said Jennifer.

"Yes, it is," said Papa, leaning back on the heels of his black cowboy boots. "But I'm just happy that they built this great museum to honor the game!"

Mimi looked at her watch. "I need to meet some folks in the library," she said. "You kids watch the movie and look around. I'll text you when I'm done. Papa, would you like to come with me?"

"Anything I can do to help my mystery-writing Mimi!" Papa said, waving to the kids. "Stay out of trouble!"

"Us?" said Grant. "Why would you say that to us?"

Everyone laughed.

"OK," said Christina. "The Grandstand Theater is this way. Let's go learn more about the history of baseball!"

As Christina swung around to head in the direction of the theater, she noticed a man standing behind a glass exhibit case. *Why is he wearing sunglasses in here?* she thought. *And why do I feel like he is staring at us?* She quickly looked away and followed the other kids. But her stomach flipped, and she had the feeling she would see him again.

7
BABE RUTH ROCKS!

The kids strolled out of the small theater at the museum. They had just watched a movie about the history of baseball.

"Those old players were really OLD!" said Grant. "And they sure talked a lot about Babe Ruth," he added, eyeing Christina.

"They sure did!" Christina replied. She was proud to have Babe's baseball card in her backpack.

As the kids walked past the timeline exhibits about baseball, Jennifer stopped to read a sign. "In the first baseball games in America, pitchers threw underhanded and the balls were softer. That's like softball!"

"And no one wore gloves," Christina remarked.

"It would hurt to catch without a glove!" said Grant. He squatted down into a catcher's stance. He caught and then threw an imaginary ball to Roberto.

"The bases were farther apart than they are now," said Jennifer.

"Hmmm," said Christina. "The first team to score 21 runs won!"

"That would take forever!" cried Grant.

"This says it only took a couple of innings back then," said Christina. "Then in 1857, the rules started changing. They made a game last for nine innings. The bases were set 90 feet apart, like they are today."

"Look at this!" cried Grant. "You could put a runner out by throwing the ball and hitting him with it! I'm sure glad they changed THAT rule!"

Grant pretended to throw a ball right at Roberto. Roberto clutched his arm and tumbled to the ground. Jennifer gestured like an umpire and shouted, "You're out!"

"The first professional team was the Cincinnati Red Stockings," said Christina. "That was in 1869."

"Professional means they were paid to play baseball, right?" asked Grant.

"Right!" said Christina.

"Look at the pictures of these old players," said Roberto.

"I like their old uniforms," said Jennifer. "It reminds me of your Babe Ruth card, Christina." The kids peered at photographs of old players like Honus Wagner, Ty Cobb, Cy Young, Mickey Mantle, and Lou Gehrig.

"Look, you guys!" exclaimed Christina. "There's a whole room on Babe Ruth."

A tour guide stood inside the room. "Come on in, kids," she said. "Learn about Babe Ruth, one of baseball's most recognizable stars!"

Christina clutched her backpack as they walked through the room. The guide told them Babe Ruth's real name was George Herman Ruth. He was called "the Babe" and "the Bambino." He started out as a pitcher with the Boston Red Sox. Later, they moved him to the outfield.

"He was the first star baseball player," said the guide. "In 1919, he led the major leagues with 29 home runs. It was the first time any player had hit more than 25 home runs in a season."

The guide told them the Red Sox traded Babe to the New York Yankees in 1919. "As a Yankee," said the guide, "Babe became the greatest home run hitter the game had ever seen! His record of 714 home runs stood until Hank Aaron broke it in 1974."

"Wow!" said Grant, clearly impressed. "Babe Ruth rocks! Maybe you have a pretty good baseball card, after all, Christina."

Christina gazed at a worn, brown baseball glove in a display case. It was the glove "the Babe" wore during the 1926 season.

Christina glanced at Jennifer who was standing near her. Jennifer's eyes were closed. She was mumbling something.

"What are you doing?" Christina asked.

"I'm memorizing Babe Ruth's stats!" replied Jennifer. "He had 714 home runs, 2,213 runs batted in, and a .342 batting average. As a pitcher, he had 94 wins and 46 losses, an earned run average of 2.28, and 488 strikeouts."

Christina grinned. "You are a walking computer, Jennifer!" she said.

"That's my sister!" said Roberto.

As they left the Babe Ruth room, Grant stooped down to pick up something. "The Babe is EVERYWHERE!" he said, handing a dirty piece of paper to Christina.

Christina read the handwriting on it.

> Babe Ruth
> Birthplace Museum,
> 216 Emory Street,
> Baltimore, Maryland

The kids looked at each other. "I'm really getting spooked," said Grant, staring at the paper.

"The Babe IS everywhere," Christina said. "But why?" She opened her backpack and put the paper next to the Babe Ruth baseball card. She zipped up the flap and slung the bag over her shoulder.

She felt like someone was watching them. But she kept that to herself—for now.

8
CHASING HANK AARON

The museum was getting crowded. Christina kept looking over her shoulder. *Is someone following us?* she thought. *Or is it only my imagination?*

"Let's stop here," said Jennifer. She stood in front of a sign that said: "Hank Aaron: Chasing the Dream."

"The Hammer!" cried Grant, swinging an imaginary bat.

"What's 'The Hammer'?" asked Christina.

"Hank Aaron!" Grant replied. "One of baseball's greatest hitters of all time!"

"Why did they call him that?" asked Christina. "So many players have nicknames!"

Papa overheard her question. "Because he kept hammering away at the ball!" he remarked.

"Hank Aaron was awesome," Jennifer explained. "He broke Babe Ruth's home run record in 1974. He ended up with 755 home runs in his career! Plus, he still holds several important baseball records like the most runs batted in, and the most extra base hits!"

"Very impressive, my dear!" Papa said. Everyone clapped. Jennifer doffed her baseball cap and made a low, sweeping bow.

"I remember the first time I saw Hank Aaron play ball," said Papa. "He was playing with the Indianapolis Clowns of the Negro American League."

"What?" said the kids in unison.

"He was a clown?" asked Grant.

"What do you mean by Negro American League?" asked Christina.

"At one time," said Papa, "African Americans were not allowed to play in the National Baseball League. They had their own leagues."

"That's ridiculous!" said Christina.

"I agree," said Papa. "Unfortunately, that's how it was back then. But Hank was so good he spent just a few years in the Negro Leagues before going to play with the Milwaukee Braves. He was with them when they became the Atlanta Braves. Look, here's his locker from the old Atlanta Fulton County Stadium."

"I wonder if there are any stinky socks in it!" said Grant. "PEEE-YOU!" Grant wrinkled up his nose and giggled. Soon, he and Roberto were holding their noses.

"Stinky socks, stay away!" cried Roberto.

Suddenly, Grant got serious. "Wow!" he said. "This says he won three Gold Glove Awards."

"Look!" said Roberto. "Here's the uniform he wore when he hit his 715th career home run."

"That's when he broke the Babe's record!" said Jennifer.

"I wonder if they found the person who tried to steal his bat and ball from the museum in Atlanta," said Roberto.

"I hope no one tries to steal this stuff," said Grant, looking over his shoulder.

Christina glanced around, too. Goosebumps broke out on her arms, and she shivered.

"There's an exhibit here about the Negro American League," said Papa. "Let's go take a look at it." The kids followed Papa out of the museum room.

"Christina," whispered Grant, "is that guy following us?"

Christina spun around and looked behind them. A man carrying a black gym bag and wearing a dark blue baseball cap stopped suddenly and turned in another direction.

"The guy who just ducked behind the woman pushing a baby stroller?" asked Christina.

"Yeah," said Grant. "I think he's been following us ever since we left the Babe Ruth room. Is something going on?"

Christina didn't answer. She just grabbed Grant's arm and hurried after Papa.

9
BABE'S CLOSE CALL

Papa and the kids stood in front of the exhibit about the Negro Leagues.

"The National Baseball League was formed in 1876," said Brianna Brown, their tour guide. "In the early days, people of any race could play in it. But back then, there was a lot of discrimination in the United States. Fans and their own teammates often mistreated African American players. Team owners stopped hiring them. So black players, who were referred to as Negroes in those days, began forming their own teams."

"Where did they play?" asked Christina.

"They had to travel around," said Brianna. "Money was scarce. They didn't have their own stadiums."

"That makes me **irate**," said Christina, putting her hands on her hips.

"It was a different time," said Papa. "Jackie Robinson changed all that, though."

"Who was Jackie Robinson?" asked Grant, staring at the ballplayer's picture.

"Jackie Robinson was on a Negro team called the Kansas City Monarchs," said Brianna. "The general manager of the Brooklyn Dodgers saw Robinson play and decided to sign him to a contract. Robinson took the field for the Dodgers in 1945."

"That was a really big deal," Papa added. "Some of his teammates didn't want to play with him. Some opposing teams threatened to strike. Some white fans booed him."

"But black fans flocked to see Jackie Robinson," said Brianna. "At the end of the season, he received the very first Major League Baseball Rookie of the Year award. He was quite a baseball player!"

"That's an award you get when you're a first-year player," said Grant to the kids.

"So what happened to the Negro Leagues?" asked Roberto.

"Eventually, they died out," said Brianna. "As more African American players joined the major leagues, there was less need for the Negro Leagues."

"Isn't there an exhibit here about the Women's Baseball League?" Papa asked Brianna.

"Yes, there is," said Brianna. "Come this way. Did you girls know there was once a girl's professional baseball league?" she asked Christina and Jennifer.

All the kids shook their heads no.

"Well, I bet you'll be interested in this!" said Brianna. She led Papa and the kids to an exhibit called "Diamond Dreams: Women of Baseball."

"The All-American Girls Professional Baseball League started during World War II," said Brianna. "Lots of major league baseball players went off to war. In 1943, Chicago Cubs owner Phillip Wrigley decided to form the league. They played in the Midwest. But the rules were more like the rules of baseball than softball. So Wrigley changed the name to the All-American Girls Professional Baseball League."

Christina set her backpack down at her feet to peer more closely at the photographs of women who had played in the league. She read some of the team names: Racine Belles, Kenosha Comets, Rockford Peaches, and South Bend Blue Sox.

"Their uniforms are like baseball uniforms," said Jennifer, "except they have skirts instead of pants!"

"Women from all over the country competed for a place on the teams," said Brianna. "Men managed the teams. The women played great baseball and drew large crowds. Even after World War II ended, more teams were added to the women's league."

"Did you see them play, Papa?" asked Christina.

"Yep," said Papa. He tipped his cowboy hat off his forehead. "In fact, I saw the Kalamazoo Lassies win the league championship back in 1954."

Even Brianna looked impressed.

"What happened to the women's league?" asked Christina.

"By the end of the 1950s, it just died out," said Brianna.

Suddenly, Christina cried out. "NOOOOO!" she screamed, as someone grabbed the backpack at her feet and ran. "He's got my backpack!"

The kids started yelling. Papa and Brianna took off after the man who scrambled through the crowd. The kids followed on their heels. Christina could see the back of a dark blue baseball cap bobbing like a moving target as the man pushed his way past visitors.

"Security!" yelled Brianna.

Up ahead, Christina saw two security guards tussle with the man. One guard grabbed Christina's backpack and yanked it away. But the thief managed to escape their grasp. He knocked several people out of the way and bolted out the door.

A security guard handed Christina her backpack. "Sorry, young lady," he said. "We've alerted guards outside. Maybe they will catch him."

"That guy was following us!" said Grant. "I noticed him."

"Well, he's out of here now," said the guard. "But hang on tight to your belongings."

Christina clutched her backpack. The zipper was still closed. *The thief didn't have time to take anything out of it*, she thought. But she looked inside anyway. There was the Babe Ruth baseball card and the address. *Safe and sound for now*, she thought. *But that was a close call. I definitely have to be more careful with you, Babe.*

10
CURSES AND GHOSTS!

"Thank you so much for this personal tour," Christina told Brianna. Papa had left to find Mimi, but the tour guide had stayed with the kids. She felt bad about the incident with Christina's backpack.

"I've sure learned a lot about baseball," said Grant.

"You should visit during the haunted baseball tour," said Brianna.

"What do you mean?" asked Grant, stopping dead in his tracks.

Brianna laughed. "Oh, there are plenty of ghosts in baseball," she said. "Some people claim a lot of dead players are still looking for a game. Besides all the glory, there's a darker side of baseball, too. There are a number of legends, curses, and scandals. We talk about it during the haunted tour!"

"I don't believe in c-c-urses and gh-gh-ghosts!" replied Grant, lifting his arms like ghost rising above Jennifer's head. "OOOOOHHHH!" Jennifer giggled and brushed him away.

"Tell that to the Boston Red Sox fans!" said Brianna.

"What do you mean by that?" asked Christina.

"Have you heard of the Curse of the Bambino?" asked Brianna.

"You mean Babe Ruth?" asked Christina. Her stomach felt queasy.

"That's the Bambino!" said Brianna. "Between 1903 and 1918, the Boston Red Sox won the World Series five times. They were baseball's most successful team. In 1919, the Red Sox sold Babe Ruth's contract to the New York Yankees."

"They sold the Babe?" asked Grant.

"They did!" Brianna replied. "But after

they did, the Red Sox didn't win another World Series title for 86 years! And the Yankees went on to dominate baseball! People believe it's because the Red Sox sold Babe to the Yankees. Legends have it that Babe's ghost still roams the dark places of Fenway Park where the Red Sox play. Others see the ghost at Yankee Stadium!"

Christina shuddered.

"What about scandals?" asked Jennifer.

"The most famous scandal," said Brianna, "is the Black Sox scandal. It also happened in 1919. The Chicago White Sox were playing in the World Series against the Cincinnati Reds. Officials accused eight players of taking money from gamblers to intentionally lose. They banned the eight players from the game forever. One of those players, 'Shoeless' Joe Jackson, was one of the game's greatest hitters. But because he was kicked out of baseball, Jackson is not eligible for election to the Hall of Fame."

"Did they really throw the game?" asked Roberto.

"Who knows?" replied Brianna. "Owners took advantage of players during those days. Players weren't paid much. The owners made all the money."

"I've heard of that scandal," said Jennifer. "There was a movie about it."

"Yes," said Brianna. "It's called *Eight Men Out.* The Black Sox ghosts appear in another movie, too. It's called *Field of Dreams.*"

"We have that movie!" said Roberto. "Some guy builds a baseball field on his farm in Iowa. Shoeless Joe Jackson and other players appear out of the cornfield at night to play ball."

"That's right!" said Brianna. "Now, there are other dark things in baseball, too. For example, it seems that thieves are constantly stealing baseball memorabilia to sell on the black market."

Christina clutched her backpack tighter. This talk about ghosts and curses was making her nervous. She even felt like Babe Ruth was trying to tell her something.

He's just a baseball card in my backpack, she thought. *But it's a backpack someone tried to steal!* said a voice in her head.

11
FOLLOW ME!

Nearly 300 bronze plaques gleamed from the walls of the baseball museum's Hall of Fame Gallery.

"Usually, only a couple of players make the Hall of Fame each year," said their tour guide Brianna. "There's one plaque for each person honored. The Hall honors players, managers, and other people closely associated with the game.

"A player has to have played at least ten seasons of ball to be considered for election," she continued. "And he has to have been retired for five years. There's only been one exception to that rule so far."

"Roberto Clemente," said Jennifer softly. She and Roberto stood in front of the plaque of the Pittsburgh Pirate right fielder.

"That's right," said Brianna. "They waived the rule, because Clemente died while he was still a player."

"Yeeoowww!" Grant suddenly cried. Christina spun around. Grant sat on the marble floor, rubbing his shoulder. He stared up at a life-sized statute of a player dressed in a Yankee pinstripe uniform with a number 3 on his back.

Christina walked over to look up at the player's face. But she already knew who it was—Babe Ruth! His bat was poised to swing as he stared straight ahead at an imaginary pitcher.

"Babe Ruth," said Brianna, "was in the first group of five players to be inducted into the Hall of Fame."

Christina reached down to help Grant get up. "We should've known you'd run into the Babe," she said and giggled.

"At least it's not his ghost!" said Grant, rubbing his backside.

Christina and Grant walked over to Babe Ruth's plaque. Just then, they overheard Brianna talking to another guide. "Is that the young lady whose backpack was snatched?" asked the other guide. Brianna nodded. "Well, a baseball jersey has disappeared from an exhibit. We don't know if it was the same person or not."

The two guides started to whisper.

"Did you hear that?" asked Grant.

"Yeah," said Christina. "It's odd. Everywhere we go, something gets stolen."

"AND someone tried to steal your backpack," said Grant.

"I know," replied Christina. "It doesn't add up." She looked at her watch. "It's almost time to meet Mimi and Papa. Let's go play some games in the kid's area."

The kids thanked Brianna and ran over to the Sandlot Kids' Clubhouse. The exhibit was full of interactive games geared toward young fans.

"I love Curious George," said Grant, watching "Curious George Plays Baseball" on a television monitor. Grant and Roberto relaxed in two chairs that looked like huge baseball mitts. "He's just so...curious!" said Roberto. The two boys giggled.

Christina and Jennifer opened old-style, wooden knothole locker doors to see the baseball artifacts hidden behind each. CREEEEEEEEEEK!!

"Wow, that's a noisy one!" said Jennifer.

"It's almost spooky," agreed Christina as she opened it.

She inspected an old jersey hanging on a hook. Then she picked up a worn baseball. Underneath the baseball was an old spiral notebook. Christina flipped open the cover of the notebook. She gasped!

"GRANT!" she yelled. "Get over here!"

Grant and the other two kids huddled around Christina as she read a note stuck to the front page of the notebook.

Go to where

the curse was born.

"I think our mystery is getting more mysterious," said Grant.

Christina carefully tore the page with the note from the spiral notebook. She put the newest note with her other clues. Behind her, she felt a sudden cool breeze. She thought she heard a voice whisper in her ear, "Follow me!"

12
GOTTA LOVE LITTLE LEAGUE!

Soon after landing at the airport in Williamsport, Pennsylvania, Papa, Mimi, and the kids were walking into the Peter J. McGovern Little League Museum in South Williamsport. The red brick building sat between two Little League baseball fields. Crowds filled the stands. Banners hung on fences. Teams of sweaty boys in red, blue, gold, and green uniforms dotted the fields or milled around anxiously awaiting their game time. It was noisy! It was exciting! It was the Little League Baseball World Series!

"Cool!" said Grant. He and Roberto wore their team's red baseball caps and jerseys. Jennifer's ponytail peeked out of her light blue softball hat.

"Would you like me to buy you a baseball cap, Christina?" asked Mimi.

"That's OK," said Christina, flipping her stick-straight hair. "I don't like hats."

Grant, Roberto, and Jennifer looked at her with their hands on their hips.

"But you guys look great!" Christina said. "Hats just mess up my hair!"

"Enough about your hair," Grant said. "I'm ready to play ball!" He picked up a bat and swung it. Then he watched his swing in the instant replay monitor. "Pretty good form, don't you think?" he asked.

Papa peered at a glass case filled with old cleats. "I remember wearing these metal spikes," he said. "My teammate, Freddie Johnson, got a really bad cut from one. Needed twenty-two stitches."

"What happened?!" cried Grant.

"Well," said Papa, "he came sliding feet first into second base. Right into the other team's second baseman. The kid jumped up to catch the ball and stomped down on Freddie's leg. Tore right through his sock. Started bleeding like crazy."

"That must have hurt!" cried Grant. "But I'll bet he had a cool scar!"

"I'm sure glad they make plastic cleats now," Papa said, tugging on Grant's baseball cap. "Much safer for you boys."

They walked around looking at all the exhibits. They saw the original home plate used in the first Little League World Series game in 1959. They inspected a giant mural of the crowd at the beginning of the 1982 Little League World Series game.

"Look at this ball," said Roberto. "It was used in the first no-hitter in Little League history."

The group watched highlights of the most exciting moments of Little League World Series games. Christina took a jog around the running track. Jennifer tried her hand as a sportscaster, describing the play-by-play action as she watched a World Series game.

"That was fun!" she said. "I might want to be a sports broadcaster some day."

"You should be!" said Christina. "You can really rattle off those statistics!"

"This is great fun," said Mimi, "but we better get out to the field. We have tickets for the next game!"

In all the excitement, Christina forgot about the baseball card in her backpack. Then she passed a glass case with a worn ball inside. She read the sign: This ball traveled more than 500 feet when Babe Ruth hit a home run in an exhibition game played in Williamsport on October 31, 1923. *Babe Ruth is everywhere,* she thought.

Just then, Christina caught a glimpse of a black bag as its owner disappeared around a corner of the room. Was it the same guy? Was that even a gym bag? She wasn't sure.

I don't know which is worse, she thought, *the ghost of Babe Ruth haunting me or strangers with black gym bags following me.* She shivered.

13
YOU THROW LIKE A GIRL!

The kids were walking around, soaking up the atmosphere of the Little League World Series.

"I wished we'd been playing in that game," said Grant to Roberto.

"I know," Roberto replied. "Watching it made me want to play! Let's go find one of their practice fields. I bet someone will let us play for a while."

"I think I'll go sit with Mimi and Papa," said Christina.

"No, come with us," said Jennifer.

"Yeah, come with us, Christina," said Grant. "Don't be afraid to hit a ball!"

"I'm not afraid," said Christina. "I just don't want to."

"Just think of Babe Ruth," said Roberto and giggled.

"Yeah, come on!" said Grant. "Christina's gonna' hit like Babe Ruth!"

"Let's see if we can play with those guys over there," said Roberto. The kids waved to a group of boys throwing a ball around.

"Hey, you guys!" yelled Roberto. "Can we play with you? We've got a ball and gloves but no bat."

Christina saw Grant, Roberto, and Jennifer reach into their backpacks and pull out gloves and balls. *Great! I don't have anything*, she thought.

The group of kids waved them over. After a few quick introductions, they were were playing ball like old friends.

"Here, use this," said Jennifer, tossing Christina her glove. "I'll go barehanded."

The two girls threw back and forth a few times.

"How am I doing?" asked Christina.

"Oh, OK," said Jennifer. "Except you're throwing like a girl!" She laughed. "Here, let me show you. Don't just stand flat-footed. Step into your throw—just watch this."

Jennifer turned her head to find Grant or Roberto. "Grant!" she yelled. "Let me throw the ball to you!" Jennifer tossed the baseball, demonstrating her form to Christina. "See!" she said. "Now you throw it to me."

Christina threw the ball. Roberto nodded approvingly. "That's better, Christina," he remarked.

"You guys want to bat a little?" said one of the kids on the field. "Our pitcher needs some practice."

Grant, Roberto, and Jennifer yelled "Great!" Christina hesitated.

"Come on," said Jennifer. "Hey, go easy on her. She hasn't played in a while," she said to the pitcher.

When it was Christina's turn, she whiffed the ball three times. But all the kids encouraged her, so she got in line and tried it again. The sun was low in the sky, and the day's heat was giving way to a cool evening. Christina had to admit, it was kind of fun!

WHACK! On her fourth turn, Christina's bat connected with the ball. It headed right for Grant, who was standing at the shortstop position. Christina looked shocked, then beamed with pleasure. But then, THUMP! The ball smacked Grant right in the shoulder. He twirled around and fell to the ground, flat on his back.

"OH, NO!" screamed Christina, racing to her brother. She dropped to her knees. Grant lay motionless on the ground. The ball rested next to his outstretched arm.

"Grant!" Christina cried. The other players ran over and huddled around them. Grant moaned and slowly moved his head from side to side.

"Grant, are you OK?" Christina asked. "Oh, what have I done?" She cradled her head in her hands. Suddenly, Grant's bright blue eyes flew open and he grabbed Christina's shoulders. "See, I knew you could do it!" he yelled. "After all, you're my sister!"

Grant sprang to his feet. Roberto slapped him on the back, and Grant launched his arms in the air like the champion in a heavyweight boxing match. "I'm back!" he cried. "Back in action!"

"Ohhhhhh, you!" Christina growled. "Don't scare me like that ever again!" She stalked back to home plate.

"Let me throw you a couple more," said the pitcher. Christina took a few practice swings and smacked the ball once again. This time it was a little blooper between first and second base.

DING! Just then, Christina got a text from Mimi. "Mimi says it's time for dinner," she said. The kids picked up their belongings and headed to meet Mimi and Papa at the front gate.

Once everyone finished their Italian dinner of spaghetti with meatballs, garlic bread, and salad, Papa announced he had rented a movie to watch. He handed a DVD to Christina.

"It's called *A League of their Own*," Papa said. "It's about the All-American Girls Professional Baseball League." He looked at Roberto and Grant, who were rolling their eyes. "And you boys will like it too—trust me on that."

The kids were glued to the TV for the next couple of hours.

"It would have been cool to play on that league," said Jennifer.

"Those girls were actually pretty good!" added Grant.

Mimi swept into the room, collecting drink cans and popcorn bowls. "Time for bed, everyone," she announced. "We're off to Kentucky tomorrow—bright and early—to visit another famous baseball location!"

Christina smiled. *This baseball trip is getting to be a lot of fun after all,* she thought. There was only one problem. She hadn't told Grant that she thought she saw the guy who tried to steal her backpack again this evening. He was standing by the fence at tonight's game wearing a red baseball cap. And she thought she spotted a black gym bag on the ground next to his feet.

I'm getting paranoid, thought Christina. But she really had a feeling it was the same mysterious guy!

14

BATTER UP!

Christina shaded her eyes with her hand as she looked straight up into the cloudless blue sky.

"I can't believe this!" said Jennifer.

"Neither can I," said Roberto.

Grant's mouth gaped open. For once, he was speechless!

The kids, Mimi, and Papa stood on the sidewalk next to the Louisville Slugger Museum and Factory in downtown Louisville, Kentucky. A gigantic baseball bat leaned casually against the side of the five-story brick building. The bat was a whole story taller than the building it rested against.

"That is one enormous bat!" Mimi exclaimed. She opened a brochure about the museum. "This bat is 120 feet tall," she said. "It's an exact-scale replica of Babe Ruth's 34-inch Louisville Slugger."

Christina spun around and looked at Mimi. Grant's mouth opened wider as he shot Christina a look. "Babe Ruth!" he mouthed.

Inside the museum, Mimi took pictures of the kids giggling as they nestled in a giant baseball glove. "OK, everyone," she announced. "I need to do some research. When I come back, we'll take a tour of the factory."

"Why don't you kids try out some bats at the batting cage over there while we're gone," said Papa with a twinkle in his eye. "Maybe you'll get a surprise when we get back!"

"Yesssss!" cried Grant, jumping into one of the cages.

The kids spent the next hour swinging replicas of bats used by Babe Ruth, Ted Williams, and Derek Jeter in the museum's batting cage. Christina chose a bat like Babe used. CRAAACK! Christina hit the ball hard. CRAACK! She hit it again.

Jennifer, Roberto, and Grant clapped. Christina grinned.

"Wow!" yelled Grant. "You knocked the cover off that ball!"

"You **decimated** it!" cried Roberto.

One more time, thought Christina. CRAAACK!

Then she noticed a man leaning against the chain link fence watching them. He was tall and wore a green windbreaker. His shaggy, reddish-grey hair stuck out from under his black ball cap. *Who's that?* she thought, frowning. As they left the batting cage, he approached them, waving and grinning.

"Christina," he said, sticking out his hand. "My name is Jack LaForge. I just saw your grandpa. He said he told you kids about selling his baseball card collection to me. This must be Grant and Roberto and Jennifer!"

Christina shook his hand, relieved that he was an acquaintance and not someone else following them. *I'm really getting suspicious of people*, she thought.

"Did you give Papa a million dollars for his baseball cards?" asked Grant.

"No, no!" said Jack LaForge and laughed. "But he had some good cards." He turned to Christina. "I saw you swinging a bat like the one Babe Ruth used," he said. Jack LaForge pointed to a glass case with a bat in it. "Here's a bat he actually played with during his 60-home-run season in 1927."

The kids stared. "Do you like Babe Ruth?" he asked.

"Let's just say, we've learned a lot about him on this trip," Christina replied.

"Here's a bat Joe DiMaggio used during his 56-game hitting streak," said LaForge. "The players really like Louisville Sluggers. Well, you kids have fun. If you get a chance, have your grandpa bring you to see my baseball memorabilia collection. I think you'd like it."

Christina watched Jack LaForge walk away. "That man looks so familiar," she murmured.

The kids walked around a corner and came face-to-face with three life-size mannequins.

"Wow!" said Jennifer. "Here's Ted Williams, Ken Griffey, Jr., and, of course, Babe Ruth!"

Christina slowly sidestepped around the mannequin of Babe Ruth.

"What's wrong with you, Christina?" Grant asked.

Christina stopped and stared straight into Babe Ruth's eyes. Then she looked down at the sleeve of his New York Yankees jersey. There it was! A piece of paper barely stuck out of his sleeve. She slipped it out of its hiding place.

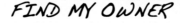

FIND MY OWNER

Christina gasped.

"What does that mean?" Roberto asked. "Find whose owner?"

Christina and Grant looked at each other, then down at the paper again.

"I think we have a ghost on our hands," whispered Christina.

15
BATS! BATS! AND MORE BATS!

The kids, Mimi, and Papa set out on a guided tour through the factory at the Louisville Slugger Museum and Factory.

"Louisville Slugger is the official bat of Major League Baseball," said the tour guide. "The first bat was made in 1884. Now, we make about one million bats a year. On a busy day, we make about 1,500 bats at this factory."

Chips of wood flew through the air as craftspeople, wearing goggles, cut bats down to size. Other workers used sandpaper to smooth the bats. Another group stamped the bats with the famous Louisville Slugger logo. Hundreds of bats hung from racks drying. Bats in all sizes, as well as special edition bats, were stacked for shipment.

The tour guide showed them bins labeled with the names of major league ballplayers. Each bin held a stack of pre-cut lumber. When a player needed a new supply of bats, all he had to do was call!

"Look!" said Grant. "There's a bin ready for Derek Jeter and another one for Albert Pujols!"

"Is it true a professional player goes through about one hundred bats during a season?" asked Jennifer.

"That's right!" said the tour guide. "We make more than 8,000 types of bats. Every player's bat is custom made. You probably saw the replica of Babe's 34-inch bat leaning against the building. Hank Aaron used a bat similar to Babe Ruth's except his was a little longer and weighed less. Mickey Mantle used a medium handle and a small to medium barrel."

"Mickey Mantle, centerfielder and first baseman for the New York Yankees," said Jennifer. "He won the American League's Most Valuable Player Award three times! He also played in sixteen All-Star games, twelve World Series, and holds the record for the most home runs hit in the World Series!"

"Jennifer, you continue to amaze me!" said Mimi.

"What kind of wood do you use?" Papa asked the tour guide.

"Bats are mostly made from northern white ash or maple," the guide replied.

At the end of the tour, Papa revealed his surprise. "Each of you can pick out a bat! We'll have your name put on it."

Grant and Roberto high-fived. Jennifer beamed. Even Christina grinned.

"Do you want a bat, Christina?" Grant asked incredulously.

"Yes!" said Christina. "I believe I do!"

Later, when the bats were ready, Mimi and Papa gave the kids another surprise. They each posed for a picture with their bat. Then, the photographer made each of them an All-Star baseball card with their picture on it.

"Now THIS is a collector's item!" said Christina, holding up her card.

"Maybe that Jack man will want to buy mine someday," said Grant, "when I'm rich and famous!"

Just then, their tour guide walked up. "It was fun showing you through the factory," he said. "But we have to ask you to leave now. We are closing early for the day. Someone just stole some replica bats."

Christina tightened her hand on the strap of her backpack. She had not noticed the man with the black gym bag anywhere. But it was crowded. She gave Grant a sideways glance. He shook his head and shrugged his shoulders. "I haven't seen anything strange," he whispered. "But SOMETHING is going on!"

16

SHOELESS JOE AND THE BLACK GYM BAG

"OK, we need to talk about this mystery," said Christina, her new bat resting between her knees. The kids were sitting on a bench waiting their turn to bat at a batting cage near their hotel.

"What are our clues?" asked Grant.

"First, I found the Babe Ruth baseball card," said Christina.

"Then I found the piece of paper with the address for the Babe Ruth Birthplace and Museum on it," said Grant.

"And how about that weird note you found in that old locker?" asked Jennifer.

Christina opened her backpack. "It says, 'Go to where the curse was born,'" she said. "Then this last note says, 'Find my owner.' I know this sounds crazy, but I think Babe Ruth is talking to me."

"That's CREEEPY!" said Roberto.

"If it were true, it would mean there *are* ghosts!" said Grant, his eyes wide with alarm.

"That tour guide said there are plenty of ghosts in baseball," said Christina. "Also, I think someone is following us. I think I've seen the same guy a couple of times, carrying a black gym bag. I think it's the same thief who almost snatched my backpack."

"Plus, everywhere we go, something gets stolen!" said Grant.

Just then, it was their turn to hit. Soon, they were taking turns swinging their new bats. Christina chose the slowest pitching machine. She concentrated on the ball and connected on nearly every ball the pitching machine sent her way. "Wooo hooo!" she cried. "I really am starting to like this baseball stuff!"

"Have you ever seen the movie *Field of Dreams*?" asked Jennifer as they walked back to the hotel.

"No," said Christina. "That's the one the tour guide Brianna talked about, right?"

Jennifer nodded. "A corn farmer in Iowa keeps hearing voices that urge him to build a baseball field right in his cornfields," she explained. "Shoeless Joe Jackson and some of his Black Sox teammates suddenly appear to play on the field. It's all very mysterious!"

"And full of ghosts!" said Roberto to Grant, elbowing him in the ribs.

"Yikes!" cried Grant.

That night, Christina dreamed she was standing in a cornfield. Shoeless Joe tossed his bat to her and told her to take a swing at the ball. He said, "I know you can hit it out of the park!" But as a pitcher threw a blazing fastball right at her, Christina saw the man with the black gym back reaching for her backpack.

She woke up in a cold sweat.

17
LONG BALLS AND GHOSTS

The famous Fenway Park in Boston, Massachusetts, was fairly empty. The Boston Red Sox team was playing in Baltimore. Only a few fans milled around, touring the one-hundred-year-old stadium. The kids sat in the upper right field stands. Mimi and Papa were meeting with a baseball historian just below their seats.

"Fenway Park is the oldest baseball stadium in America," said Christina. She was reading from her Boston guidebook. "It opened in 1912."

"Why is this the only red seat?" asked Grant. He was sitting in Fenway Park's "Lone

Red Seat." The seat stood out in a sea of green bleachers.

"Red Sox left fielder Ted Williams hit the longest home run ever hit at Fenway Park right at this seat," read Christina. "The distance was officially measured at 502 feet from home plate. It says if the ball hadn't hit this seat, it probably would have gone a lot farther."

"I wish I'd been sitting here when he blasted that ball!" said Grant.

"The ball hit a man in the head," said Christina. "He didn't even catch it. The sun was in his eyes. It bounced higher into the bleachers."

Grant jerked his body back as if a ball had hit him. He stood up and started weaving around. "Ohhhh, I have such a headache," he mumbled. The kids laughed.

"It also says Babe Ruth hit some long home runs balls here that landed across the street from center field," said Christina. "They think his balls went 500 feet or more."

"So Babe Ruth actually played in this stadium," said Jennifer.

"Yes!" said Christina. "It says he was a pitcher here the first year he played."

"Doesn't the baseball card you have say he's a pitcher?" asked Grant.

Christina took the card out of her backpack. "Yes, it does," she said.

"Then that is his rookie card," remarked Grant, pointing to the baseball card.

"What does that mean?" asked Christina.

"They make a new card each season," explained Jennifer. "So this card is from the first year he played. It's his rookie card!"

"The Curse of the Bambino started here, right?" asked Roberto.

"That's right," said Christina. "It started when the Boston Red Sox sold Babe Ruth to the New York Yankees."

"I wonder if he was mad about going to the Yankees," said Roberto. "Do you think he put a spell on the Red Sox?"

"I wonder if his ghost really walks around here," said Grant. He started looking over his shoulder and under the seats.

"I doubt it," said Christina. But she felt a prickle of excitement. "Let's walk around and see if we can find something spooky!" she said and giggled.

"See that big green wall out in left field?" asked Jennifer. "They call that the Green Monster. It's the highest wall in any major league baseball park."

"Wow!" said Grant. "People sit on top of that thing! I wonder if they ever catch home runs up there!"

Clouds covered up the sun as they walked behind the stands. Shadowy fingers played mysteriously across the walls of the **corridor**. The wind blew eerily.

"It's kind of spooky here," whispered Grant. He and Roberto were walking side by side behind the girls.

"It's just old," said Christina. "Think of all the history that's there. Think how many great players have come here to play."

"You sound like Papa and Mimi now, Christina," said Grant.

The wind around them began to feel a little cooler.

"Christina!" whispered Grant. "Roberto and I think someone is following us."

Something made Christina clutch her backpack tighter. Just then, they turned a corner and looked down a long, shadowy corridor. At the end of the corridor, they spied the back of a player ambling along. He wore an old-style uniform and carried a bat. Slowly, he turned around and looked straight at them.

"It's Babe Ruth!" gasped Christina.

Fear stricken, Grant, Roberto, and Jennifer snapped around and fled back down the corridor. But Christina stood frozen in her tracks.

A dark figure stepped out of the shadows and into the space between her and the Babe. The dark figure peered in the direction of Babe Ruth, who still stood silently watching them. Then, the figure bolted across the corridor and away from Christina.

The Babe tipped his cap at Christina and disappeared into thin air.

18
BALL MITTS AND SLUGGERS

Papa had flown everyone in the *Mystery Girl* to Baltimore so Mimi could visit Oriole Park at Camden Yards. The stadium was preparing for tonight's baseball game with the Boston Red Sox.

"This is a cool ballpark," said Christina. She and the kids were touring the stadium with Mimi and Papa.

"It is!" said Mimi. "It was built in the 1990s, but it was designed to look and feel like a ballpark built in the early 1900s."

"My Baltimore guidebook says Babe Ruth's father once owned a saloon on this land," said Christina.

Grant, Roberto, and Jennifer looked at Christina.

"Maybe we can find his father's ghost," Grant whispered to Christina. He rolled his eyes.

Mimi looked at her watch. "Papa and I need to go to our meeting," she said. "We will be right in that office over there. You can buy some lunch and wait for us in the stands." She handed Christina some money. "If you need anything, text me."

"We'll be fine," said Christina. "Let's get some hot dogs," she said to the kids. At the concession stand, they bought hot dogs, French fries, peanuts, and drinks.

"ARUMPPP!" said Grant, stuffing peanuts in his mouth. "I'm starved!" He turned a ketchup bottle upside down and squeezed. Ketchup spurted all over the counter and himself. "Whoops!" he said, wiping ketchup from his face. "Man, I've gone this whole trip without getting food on me. Now, look at my shirt!" Ketchup dripped down the Atlanta Braves logo on his t-shirt.

Christina dipped a napkin in her cup of ice water and rubbed out some of the ketchup stains.

"We have to have a discussion," she said.

"I knew this was coming!" cried Grant. "Christina, I don't want to see anymore ghosts of dead ball players."

"We have to go to Babe Ruth's birthplace," Christina said. "Those are our clues. We have to go to where the 'curse was born.' Babe Ruth was born in a house just a couple blocks away. We have the address." She pulled the piece of paper from her backpack. "See!" she said. "The address is 216 Emory Street, Baltimore. My guidebook says his birthplace is just a 'long fly ball away' from here!"

"We better get going then," said Grant, "and get back here quick before Mimi catches us!"

At the Babe Ruth Birthplace Museum, the kids hurriedly looked at the exhibits.

"This place sure is tiny," said Jennifer as they walked through the historic home. They looked at photos of Babe's parents, his wife, and his daughters. Grant lay **supine** across the bed in the bedroom where Babe was born.

"This is sure a tiny bed!" he squealed.

"Grant, get off of that," said Christina gruffly. "Get serious! There is something here for us. I just know it. But we have to find it."

They walked into the living room just as two men emerged from a back room. One man had shaggy hair and wore a green jacket. Christina jumped when she noticed some type of black bag slung over his shoulder. Jack LaForge looked as surprised to see the kids as they were to see him.

"You DO like Babe Ruth, don't you?" said Jack.

"We just love baseball history," said Christina, nervously fingering the strap of her backpack. She couldn't tear her eyes away from his black bag. She could only see part of it.

"Well, someone else does, too," said Jack. "Someone just tried to steal one of Babe's jerseys. Luckily, the guy didn't get away with it, though."

"Is your grandpa here?" Jack asked Christina.

"No, he and Mimi are over at Oriole Park," Christina replied as coolly as possible.

"Well, tell him I said hello again!" said Jack, waving goodbye.

"WOW!" said Grant. "Number one, we are SOOO busted! Number two, someone just tried to steal something here! And number three, Papa's friend was carrying a black bag—maybe that gym bag!"

Christina shuddered. "We need to find what we're here for and get out of here," she said. "Let's keep searching."

Christina's eyes peered over everything. *I know there is something here*, she thought. She looked into a glass case filled with old baseball artifacts. Her eyes lingered on Babe's childhood catcher's mitt. Then, she spied the clue! A piece of rolled-up paper was stuffed between the wood frame doors of the case.

"Ah ha!" said Christina. She carefully slid the paper out from between the two doors.

She unrolled it as the kids looked over her shoulder.

"SLUGGER" B.R.

Jennifer pondered the clue. "A slugger," she said, "is a baseball player who consistently hits for power, especially home runs and doubles."

"So 'Slugger' B.R. must mean the Slugger is Babe Ruth," said Christina. "But now what? It doesn't make sense."

"Nothing makes sense," said Grant. "Like how did it get here?"

The four kids looked around. The room was empty. Then they felt a rush of cold air.

"I don't know," said Christina, her hands shaking. "But this is our clue. Now, we need to get out of here!"

19

NEW YORK! NEW YORK!

Papa steered the *Mystery Girl* to New York City. Christina could see Mimi's short blond hair swinging as she sang "New York, New York" with Papa. New York City was one of Mimi and Papa's favorite places to go.

Roberto, Jennifer and Grant were excited too. Roberto and Jennifer's cousin Antonio lived in the Bronx. He had called to see if they could play a couple of innings of baseball with his team at Yankee Stadium tonight before the Yankees game. The team was short on players.

"You kids should really enjoy this opportunity," Papa remarked. "This is the chance of a lifetime."

"Are you all right with the three of us playing, Christina?" asked Jennifer.

"Of course, I am," said Christina, hiding her disappointment. "I would be scared to death to play ball at Yankee Stadium. But you guys will do great."

"GREAT!" said Grant, Roberto, and Jennifer in unison.

"Let's look at the clues for the mystery," Grant whispered. He still was worried about Christina's feelings. "Maybe we can figure something out."

Christina opened her backpack. She gently pulled out the old baseball card and the other clues.

"We agree that this is a Babe Ruth rookie card," said Christina. She placed the piece of paper with the address next to the baseball card. Then she laid down the clue that said, "Go to where the curse was born." Then she added the clue that read: "Find my owner."

"It seems like these last three clues got us to Babe's birthplace museum," said

Christina. "But then we find a clue that just seems to describe Babe Ruth: 'Slugger' B.R."

"Well, I don't get it," said Grant, taking off his baseball cap.

"You've go-ott hat head," sang Roberto. "You've go-ott hat head!"

"Do not!" said Grant. He looked at his reflection in a window of the *Mystery Girl*. "OOOOHHH! Do to!" he moaned. He shoved his cap back on his head.

"Let's watch the movie *The Natural*," Grant said. "Maybe something will come to us." He opened the lid on the DVD player and plopped the movie on the spindle.

"Yeah, let's do it," said Christina, placing the clues in her backpack.

By the time the New York City skyline appeared in the distance, slugger Roy Hobbs, The Natural, was smashing a homerun out of the park and fireworks were exploding.

Christina felt like she was running the bases, too—only she wasn't getting anywhere at all. And the only fireworks exploding were in her head.

Help me out, Babe, she thought. *Help me blast this mystery into smithereens.* A chill went up her spine. "Help me! Help me!" she said to herself.

She zipped up her backpack and stepped off the plane in New York City.

20
THE HOUSE THAT BABE BUILT

"Wow! I can't believe I'm in Yankee Stadium!" said Roberto.

"Me either!" said Grant. The two boys stood with their hands on their hips. They gazed at the stadium around them.

It was a sunny day in New York City. The light tan, limestone exterior of the stadium popped against the blue sky. The infield grass was emerald green. Colorful banners waved in the light breeze.

Jennifer pushed her Yankee ball cap back from her eyes. "I can't wait to get out on the field," she said.

Mimi, Papa, Christina, Grant, Roberto, and Jennifer had visited the Yankees Museum.

They had looked at all the Yankee baseball artifacts and memorabilia. Now, they were strolling around the grounds of the stadium.

"Did they really tear down the old Yankee Stadium?" asked Christina.

"They sure did," said Papa. "It was shortly after they opened this one in 2009. The old one was right across the street."

"Did you ever see a game in the old stadium?" asked Roberto.

"We did!" said Mimi. "I was sad when they demolished it. It held a lot of good memories for a lot of people. That's why the design of this stadium resembles the old one."

"Yep!" said Papa. "They wanted it to look as much like 'The House that Ruth Built' as possible!'"

"What do you mean by 'The House that Ruth Built'?" asked Grant. "I didn't know Babe Ruth BUILT Yankee Stadium!"

"That was a nickname for the old Yankee Stadium," said Mimi. "It was built in 1923. By then, Ruth was a baseball superstar for the Yankees. His best years coincided with the Yankees' winning history."

Just then, the group walked into the area known as Monument Park. It was something of an outdoor museum featuring plaques, monuments, and retired numbers of famous Yankee players.

"What's a retired number?" asked Grant. He stood before a row of big black numbers mounted over plaques explaining each one.

"That means no Yankee player can ever wear that number again," said Jennifer.

"See, they retired Reggie Jackson's number 44," said Mimi. "And here is Whitey Ford's number 16."

"I know Mickey Mantle," said Roberto. "He was number 7."

"Here is Joe DiMaggio's number 5," said Mimi, "and Lou Gehrig's number 4, and Babe Ruth's number 3. They were all great Yankee players."

"Most of these monuments were moved here from the old Yankee Stadium," said Papa.

Just then the group stopped in front of a large marble and bronze monument to Babe Ruth. "I read an article describing how they moved Babe's monument over here," said Papa. "They had trouble taking out the bolts. Some of the men doing the work said they didn't think Babe wanted to leave the old stadium."

Christina felt a chill go down her spine.

"I wonder if his ghost likes roaming around over here," said Jennifer.

"What do you mean?" asked Grant. He spun around and looked at Jennifer. "I thought Babe Ruth's ghost roamed around Fenway Park!"

"They say he roams both places!" said Mimi. "Ghosts have no boundaries!" She laughed.

"Maybe he's gone since they tore down the old stadium," said Grant, looking around.

"Who knows," said Mimi. "But if he's around, he may be confused!"

I think he's around here, thought Christina. She looked into the face of Babe Ruth staring from his monument. *In fact, I'm certain of it.*

What Christina didn't realize was that a shadowy figure was watching their every move.

21

BASEBALL IS JUST LIKE LIFE!

Christina sat alone in the bleachers at Yankee Stadium. Mimi had left to do some more research before the game. Papa had gone to get a hot dog at a nearby stand. Worst of all, Grant, Roberto, and Jennifer were down in the Yankee locker room. Antonio's team had arrived on a bus. They were getting ready to play ball.

I'm trying to be a good sport about this, thought Christina. *But why do I feel so sad? I've never wanted to play baseball. I would look foolish playing at Yankee Stadium.*

Just then, an elderly lady made her way into the near-empty stands. Her short white hair stuck out from under her dark blue

Yankee ball cap. She sat down in front of Christina and opened up a bag of popcorn.

She looked back at Christina. "Hi, honey," she said. "You're here awfully early."

"I've come to see my little brother and some friends play ball," Christina replied.

"Oh, I do enjoy those games with the Little Leaguers," the lady said. She stuck out her hand to Christina. "I'm Dottie!" she said.

Christina shook her hand. "I'm Christina, ma'am," she replied.

"You don't sound like you're from New York," said Dottie. "I'd say you are from the South!"

"Yes ma'am," said Christina. "I'm from Georgia."

"I didn't think I recognized you," Dottie continued. "I know a lot of the people who sit in these seats."

"My grandma is a writer," explained Christina. "She is writing a children's mystery book about baseball. She got these seats from a person at the front office."

"Do you like baseball?" asked Dottie.

"I'm liking it better," replied Christina.

"I love baseball," said Dottie. "I haven't missed a home game for 50 years. I used to play baseball, you know."

"What?" asked Christina.

"Yes," said Dottie. "I played in the All American Girls Professional Baseball League many years ago. Have you ever heard of it?"

Christina leaned forward. She was so excited! "Yes, I have heard of it!" she said. "I learned all about it at the baseball museum in Cooperstown."

"I played for the Racine Belles," said Dottie. "It was wonderful! I grew up on a farm in Indiana with a bunch of brothers. They always let me play ball with them. They taught me how to catch and bat and throw."

"You mean you don't throw like a girl?" asked Christina.

"Not even close!" said Dottie. She and Christina started to giggle.

"Anyway, my brothers went off to fight in World War II," Dottie continued. "I was going to work in a factory. One day, some men came to town to try out girls for the team. I knew I could make the team—and I did! We traveled and played baseball. I had barely been 50 miles from the farm in my whole life! It was such an exciting time and our team was really good!"

"It sounds like great fun!" said Christina.

"I played until the league folded," Dottie added. "Toward the end, we just played exhibition games. Sometimes, we just played a couple of innings, like your brother is doing today. I've never gotten over my love for baseball. I moved here to New York City with my husband many years ago. We used to come to baseball games together. I'm kind of a famous person in the crowd here. They give me free popcorn. Want some?"

Christina cupped her hands, and Dottie filled them with puffs of white popcorn.

"So why aren't you playing in this game, Christina?" asked Dottie. "I've seen girls play in them before."

"Oh, they didn't ask me," said Christina. "I'm not very good."

Dottie looked at her. Her bright blue eyes twinkled. "Can you catch the ball?" she asked, smiling.

"I'm improving," said Christina.

"Can you bat?" she said, pointing to the Louisville Slugger between Christina's knees.

"My batting is really getting pretty good," said Christina.

"Do you throw like a girl?" asked Dottie. They both laughed.

"Well, a little!" said Christina.

"You know, Christina," said Dottie. "Not everyone gets a chance to step out onto the diamond at Yankee Stadium. I wish I had gotten the chance. AND you know what they say about baseball? Baseball is just like life. Sometimes you have to step up to the plate!"

Dottie put her arm around Christina's shoulder and hugged her. Just then, Christina realized there was something she had to do.

"Thanks, Dottie," said Christina. She jumped up and grabbed her backpack and her bat. "My grandpa is wearing a black cowboy hat. He will be here soon. And my grandma has short, blond hair. She's wearing red tennis shoes. When they get here, tell them I have gone to play baseball in Yankee Stadium!"

"That's the spirit," shouted Dottie. "Knock one out of the park!"

Christina raced to the exit.

A man wearing sunglasses and a Yankees cap watched her jaunt past him. He quickly got up from his seat. Picking up a black gym bag, he took off right behind her.

22
BULL'S EYE!

Christina saw Antonio's team come on the field.

"Grant!" Christina yelled. "Is there any way I can play with you?"

Grant spun around and looked at her. "Do you really want to?" he yelled back to Christina. "We have room for another person on the roster!"

Within a few seconds, the entire team was clapping and pointing to Christina. The coach signaled her to come down, and Christina leaped onto the field.

"Put this on over your shirt," said Jennifer, tossing Christina a Yankees t-shirt.

Soon the kids were warming up. Everyone took turns at batting practice.

"Not bad," said Coach Jones, as Christina finished her drills. "I'll start you in right field for the first inning."

Soon the umpire yelled "Play Ball!" The youth league Yankees team took to the field against the youth league Phillies to play a two-inning exhibition game. Christina ran to right field. Grant took his position at shortstop. Jennifer trotted to first base, and Roberto stepped onto the pitcher's mound.

Christina watched Roberto wind up and throw a strike to the first batter. "Oh, my gosh!" she said to herself. "I'm playing ball at Yankee Stadium! This place is HUGE!"

More and more people drifted into the stadium. The scoreboard lit up. The crowd clapped and chanted. Mimi snapped pictures.

WHACK! Christina saw Papa jump up. Then she spotted the ball. It was climbing and coming in her direction. She froze.

I have to catch it, Christina thought. *I HAVE to catch it.*

Keeping her eye on the ball, she took a step back, then another. Without looking behind her, Christina ran backward. She stretched out her right arm with her mitt open to the ball. She took a wild leap. PLOP! She snagged the ball in mid-air!

Christina saw Grant pump his fist in the air. She heard cheers from the bleachers. She threw the ball to the pitcher. *Not such a great throw,* she thought. *But the catch was good enough!*

From that point on, Christina was immersed in the game. Roberto struck the next batter out. The third Phillies batter hit a blooper over Grant's head and got to first base. The fourth batter hit a fly ball to left field that Christina's teammate dropped. One run came in, and the batter was left standing on second.

OK, one run and two outs, thought Christina. *We have to get this guy out!*

WHACK! The batter hit a hard line drive—right at Grant! He snagged it.

"Wooo hooo," yelled Christina as she ran in from the field. "Nice play, brother!" she yelled at Grant, hitting him on the back.

"Nice play, sister!" Grant yelled. "Now, let's get this run back!" he shouted as they ran into the dugout.

Roberto was the team's leadoff hitter.

"YOU'RE OUT!" shouted the umpire after Roberto's third strike. But Antonio hit a single and got on first base. Jackson, the Yankees' third baseman, also got a base hit and then Grant walked. Jennifer hit a sacrifice fly to shallow right field. One, then two runs came in. The score was 2 – 1.

It was Christina's turn to bat. She swung her Louisville Slugger a few times to loosen up. Her heart pounded in her chest.

"Just a little hit to bring me in," shouted Grant from third base.

"Go get 'em, Christina!" Mimi yelled from the stands. Mimi, Papa, and Dottie were eating popcorn and waving.

Just a little hit, she thought. *Just get on base and bring Grant in.*

WHOOSH! The ball went right past her.

"STRIKE," yelled the umpire.

That's embarrassing, thought Christina.

WHIFFFFF! This time she swung, but missed the ball.

"STRRRIKE TWO," shouted the ump.

"OK, Christina, watch the ball," she said to herself.

The ball left the pitcher's hand. *Watch it, watch it,* thought Christina.

WHACK! She hit it! The ball shot passed the Phillies shortstop and rolled out into center field. Christina was stunned.

"RUN!" screamed the kids in the dugout. She looked toward Grant. He was running wildly toward home plate.

MOVE, Christina thought. And she did! She ran as fast as she had ever run.

"RUNNNNNNN!" screamed the crowd. Christina saw the Phillies first baseman standing with one leg on the base. He was stretched out and looking out toward the field with his mitt ready to catch the ball.

THUMP! Her right foot hit the bag.

PLOP! The ball hit the first baseman's outstretched mitt.

"SAFE!" yelled the ump, crossing his arms, then spreading them out.

I just got an RBI, thought Christina. The kids in the dugout jumped up and down, screaming with delight. Mimi, Papa, and Dottie were on their feet clapping.

The next batter hit the first ball pitched to him—right at the second baseman. The ball was waiting for Christina when she arrived at second base. She was out, and the inning was over. But the Yankees were ahead 3 – 1!

Christina tossed her helmet to her coach and caught her mitt from Grant. *This is so much fun*, she thought as she raced out to right field.

But the top of the next inning was not so good for the Yankees. Grant and Jennifer executed a great double play, and Roberto struck a batter out, but the Phillies scored three runs. It was 4-3, Phillies, when Christina left right field for the bottom of the last inning.

The kids were leaning on the dugout wall and cheering on the next batter. "I need some gum," said Christina to Grant. She walked over to where she had left her backpack.

"Oh no! It's gone!" she cried. Her stomach flip-flopped.

She looked up just in time to see a man in a baseball cap hurrying away from the dugout. He carried a back gym bag and her backpack was slung over his shoulder. *It's him!* she thought. *And now he has my backpack and my Babe Ruth rookie card!* Suddenly, she understood completely. The pieces of the puzzle stopped spinning and floated into place.

Christina grabbed her Louisville Slugger, jumped out of the dugout, and leaped into the tunnel after him. By now, the man was running. He bumped into a popcorn vendor, spilling boxes everywhere. People scattered out of his way and stared as Christina raced after him with her bat.

The man looked over his shoulder and sneered. He ran faster. But so did Christina. He turned down another tunnel. Now, she was close on his heels.

"Stop—you thief!" she yelled, as they sprinted through the tunnel. "Give me back my backpack!" She saw the thief pass a Yankee player. But she was gasping for breath and couldn't yell for help. *I have to keep up with him*, she thought.

Suddenly, she realized the Yankee player wore an old pinstripe uniform. As she dashed past him, he turned toward her and smiled. It was the Babe! A sudden rush of cold air swirled around Christina. She ran faster.

As Christina neared the end of the tunnel, she heard the roar of the crowd. *We must have scored a run*, she thought. Now, she could see some of her teammates on base. It looked like Grant was up at bat.

WHACK! He hit the ball.

Just then, the thief ran out onto right field. Christina was close on his heels. He looked over his shoulder and shouted, "Get out of here, kid!"

Suddenly, Christina saw the ball sailing toward them. THRUMPP!! The ball whacked the villain in the head, knocking him to his knees!

23
THREE STRIKES AND YOU'RE OUT!

By now, the crowd was roaring. Christina's teammates raced around the diamond. Grant slid into first base. The scoreboard said 5 – 4 Yankees.

Christina stood over the thief, tightly gripping her Louisville Slugger in her hand. Security guards were running to right field toward Christina. Mimi and Papa were climbing hastily over people in the stands. Grant, Jennifer, Roberto, and all their teammates were sprinting out to right field.

Why is Jack LaForge here? thought Christina. She was startled to see the shaggy-haired man walking up with two men in trench coats.

The man with the black gym bag struggled to sit up, but two security guards grabbed his shoulders.

"This man has been stealing baseball memorabilia!" shouted Christina. "He stole a Babe Ruth rookie card from Slugger McCoy at Turner Field in Atlanta. But he dropped it, and I found it! He has been chasing me, trying to get it back. He just stole my backpack with the card in it. He's also been trying to steal something from every place we've gone."

Then, Christina turned towards the thief as security guards locked handcuffs on him. "You know," she said, glaring at the man, "life is a lot like baseball. Three strikes and you're out!"

"This man's name is Bart Black," said Jack LaForge. "And you are right, Christina. He's an unsavory character. He steals and sells baseball memorabilia on the black market. I spotted him at Turner Field. I figured he had stolen the rookie card from Slugger when Slugger told me it was gone. That card is worth half a million dollars!"

Christina, Grant, Roberto, and Jennifer gasped in unison.

"I've offered to buy it from Slugger many times," said Jack LaForge. "But he would never sell it. Slugger always carried it in his back pocket because it had belonged to his father."

"How did you know I had the rookie card?" asked Christina.

"I didn't," replied Jack. "I just kept running into you. I was following Bart Black. I didn't realize he was following you!"

"How did you figure out it belonged to Slugger?" asked Jack.

"Because one clue we found said: 'Slugger' B.R," said Christina. "We thought it meant Babe Ruth was a 'slugger.' But it really meant Slugger McCoy."

"What clues?" asked Jack LaForge.

"So, you didn't write the clues we found?" asked Christina.

"I didn't write any clues," said Jack LaForge, shaking his shaggy head.

Christina, Grant, Jennifer, and Roberto looked at each other.

"The Bambino?" whispered Grant, wide-eyed.

24

NO GHOSTS ALLOWED

The FBI agents and the stadium guards escorted the handcuffed Bart Black out of the stadium.

Christina picked up her backpack, and everyone walked toward the Yankees dugout. Yankee players were emerging from their locker room.

"Look, there's Derek Jeter!" said Roberto. Jeter waved to the kids and gave them a thumbs up.

"Will you return the Babe Ruth card to Slugger McCoy for me, Mr. LaForge?" Christina asked.

"Actually, you can return it yourself," said Jack LaForge and smiled. He turned toward the stands.

Slugger McCoy stepped down out of the stands to meet the kids. He took off his frayed Atlanta Braves baseball cap and bowed to Christina.

Christina opened her backpack and removed the baseball card. She gazed at it one last time. *Is that a twinkle in his eye?* she thought.

Christina handed the rookie card to Slugger McCoy. Tears welled up in his eyes as he gave her a hug.

"Thanks for keeping it safe," he said. "This card is very special to me."

Mimi put her arm around Christina. "Well, you had a good day, you mystery-solving, baseball-playing girl!" she said. "AND I think everyone learned a lot about the game of baseball!"

"We learned that baseball is a lot like life," said Christina.

"You have to keep your eye on the ball!" said Jennifer, winking at Christina.

"And sometimes you hit a home run!" shouted Grant.

"But sometimes a walk is as good as a hit!" added Roberto.

"But most of all," said Christina, " we learned you have to get into the game!"

"I have an idea," said Papa. "Why don't we watch a Yankees game on the East Coast tonight and then fly the *Mystery Girl* to the West Coast for a game at Dodger Stadium in California? Two coasts, two iconic baseball stadiums!"

Grant crossed his arms across his chest. "Did Babe Ruth ever play for the Dodgers?" he asked.

"No," said Papa.

"Then, there's no chance we'll run into his ghost at Dodger Stadium, right?" asked Grant.

"Right!" said Christina.

"Then, California here we come!" shouted Grant, pumping his fist in the air.

With that, the major league New York Yankees and Philadelphia Phillies took their places on the field. The crowd cheered. Once again, it was time to "Play Ball!"

Well, that was fun!

Wow, glad we solved that mystery!

Where shall we go next?

EVERYWHERE!

The End

Now...go to
www.carolemarshmysteries.com
and...

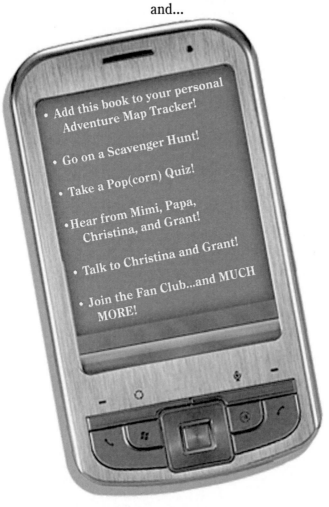

- Add this book to your personal Adventure Map Tracker!

- Go on a Scavenger Hunt!

- Take a Pop(corn) Quiz!

- Hear from Mimi, Papa, Christina, and Grant!

- Talk to Christina and Grant!

- Join the Fan Club...and MUCH MORE!

GLOSSARY

batting average: a measure of a batter's performance obtained by dividing the total of base hits by the number of times at bat, not including walks

demolished: to tear down (past tense)

doffed: to take off (past tense)

gingerly: very cautiously or carefully

immersed: deeply involved in a particular interest; or covered completely with water

memorabilia: things valued or collected for their relation to a particular field of interest

pilgrimage: a journey

replica: a close reproduction, or copy

SAT GLOSSARY

corridor: a long passage in a building, often with doors to rooms opening into it

decimate: to destroy a large part of something

irate: angry

misnomer: a wrong or unsuitable name

supine: lying on one's back with the face upward

Enjoy this exciting excerpt from:

THE MYSTERY AT Motown

1
WHAT IS A MOTOWN?

"Look! There's the Ambassador Bridge!" Papa shouted as he began the *Mystery Girl's* descent into Detroit, Michigan. The little red and white airplane tipped to the right as he made a wide turn. He spoke for a minute to the air traffic controller at the Willow Run Airport where they would land.

Mimi was excited, too, and turned in her seat. "The Ambassador Bridge is the gateway to Motown," Mimi told Christina and Grant. She and Papa had been to Detroit many times, but it was still a thrill to look down on the magnificent bridge that connected the United States to Canada.

Christina and Grant often traveled with their mystery-writing grandmother. Mimi's latest book was to be set in Motown, and she was already pumped up with the excitement of beginning a new mystery. Their grandfather, Papa, flew the family wherever Mimi's mysteries took them.

Grant, who had been dozing for a while, opened his eyes and stretched. "Is the 'Mo' in Motown like 'mow,' as in, 'mow the lawn'?" he wanted to know. "Do they have a lot of grass there?"

"No, Grant," Mimi replied. She held up her hand and pointed to a spot on it. "Motown is right here."

"What, do you want a high-five, Mimi?" Christina raised her own hand to give her one.

"No," Mimi said, smiling. "I'm just showing you where Detroit is. The state of Michigan is shaped like a mitten. Residents can show people where they live by pointing to a spot on their left hand. Detroit is in the lower portion of the thumb, and is the automotive capital of the world! Motown is a nickname for the 'Motor City.'"

"Why is Detroit called the Motor City?" Grant asked.

"Well," Mimi explained, "it's because of Detroit's association with Henry Ford. His assembly line idea for automobile production changed how cars were made. Other car companies followed his idea and were also located in Detroit."

"And," Mimi added, "Motown is the home of Motown Records where the 'Motown Sound' was born."

Christina was excited. She loved music. "Is that a rock group, Mimi?" she asked.

Mimi laughed. "No, honey," she replied. "The Motown Sound was one of Detroit's great contributions to the music world."

The plane was descending, so Mimi checked her seatbelt and smoothed the skirt of her red suit so it wouldn't wrinkle. She reminded Christina and Grant to check their seatbelts too.

"Now, where was I? Oh yes, this afternoon we're going to visit the legendary Motown Museum, Hitsville U.S.A.," Mimi said. "A very good friend of mine is the curator there, and she invited us to come!"

As soon as the kids heard the word 'museum,' they groaned. They liked museums, but it was too beautiful a day to spend indoors.

"It'll be fun, I promise," Mimi said. "To set foot in the place where so many music greats recorded their hits just gives me goose bumps." Mimi slid the sleeve of her red suit jacket back so the kids could see the tiny bumps on her skin.

"FSSSSST!" Radio static cut in. "Little red and white bird, you are cleared for landing, over."

"Roger that," Papa said into his radio. He turned to wink at the kids. "We'll have a lot to see and do while we're in Detroit," Papa told them. "From here we're going to Lafayette Coney Island for Coney dogs."

"Awesome!" Grant exclaimed. "Huh? What the heck is a Coney dog?"

"Ahhh...one of my fondest memories of Detroit," Papa said. "Coney dogs are to Detroit what apple pie is to America." He closed his eyes for a second as if to savor the memory. "Anyway, they're plump, juicy hot dogs smothered in chili and onions. Oh, and they're served with another personal favorite—chili cheese fries!"

"Oh, yes," remarked Mimi, "to go along with Papa's cast iron stomach!"

Papa winked at Mimi. "Point taken," he said with a chuckle. He reached over and flicked a few switches on the dashboard.

"Now, I'm reeeeallly hungry," Grant complained. He pulled on his hair and stretched his arms wide, making his blonde hair stick up in tufts.

"Oh, now there's a surprise," Christina commented.

Papa inhaled deeply, as if he could already smell the chili and onions. "We'll be going to lunch shortly. But first, let's set the old girl down and put her to bed."

"He means the plane," Mimi said, at the quizzical look the kids gave Papa.

Christina gazed out the window at the green landscape coming closer and closer. *Motown, here we come!* she thought.

2
YANKEES AND AIRPLANES

Papa held Mimi's hand as she climbed down the steps of the *Mystery Girl*. "My friend Joe will be here any minute to meet us," Papa explained. "He's a member of the Yankee Air Museum here, where they build and restore old war planes. You'll like him a lot. He's an 86-year-old retired World War II flight officer, and he always has an entertaining story to tell."

"I love making model airplanes!" said Grant.

A green golf cart whizzed up to meet the family. Its driver wore tinted glasses and a blue Yankee Air Museum jacket and hat. He hopped out of the front seat to greet them, shaking hands with Mimi and Papa.

Grant walked right up to Joe. "I know who you are," Grant said. "Joe, right?"

"How'd you know?" Joe asked, as if surprised.

"It says so on your belt buckle," Grant replied, pointing.

"So it does," Joe laughed, patting Grant on his head. He looked at Papa. "How about a quick tour of the Yankee Air Museum, and then meet my crew?" At Papa's nod, Joe led the family across the tarmac to a massive airplane hangar.

Joe pointed towards the airport runway. "Willow Run Airport was built by the Ford Motor Company during World War II to serve as an airfield for their B-24 bomber plant," he explained. "They used Henry Ford's automotive assembly line technique, and were able to produce one B-24 every 59 minutes."

"That's a lot of planes!" Grant shouted.

Inside the building were several restored planes, and some airplane cockpit training simulators.

Grant raced to one of the simulators and peeked inside. His hands itched to touch all those dials, switches, and levers. Tossing his backpack to the floor, he hopped inside, grabbed the control wheel, and started making plane sounds. "EEEERRRRMMM!" His voice echoed loudly, and everyone slapped their hands over their ears.

Papa tapped on the outside of the cockpit door. "OK, Ace. Come out of there before our eardrums burst."

With a reluctant "Yes, sir," Grant shuffled back to join the group.

Joe motioned to the open area where his crew was working. "Please excuse our dust. We just moved into this new hangar," he said. "Our old one burned down in 2004."

"I remember reading about that fire," Papa said. "I was so happy to hear that the *Yankee Lady* bomber was saved through the heroic efforts of museum volunteers."

Joe motioned them over to his workbench. "Yes, we were very lucky indeed, but everything else inside the hanger was destroyed, including the Waco tube glider we were restoring," Joe said. "And some of us had donated our old uniforms and artifacts from

World War II to the museum. Those can never be replaced."

Grant was mesmerized, lunch totally forgotten now. "Did it take a long time to build your glider, Mr. Joe?"

"Over twelve years, Grant," Joe said.

"Gosh, that's awful!" Grant exclaimed, his eyes downcast.

Joe saw Grant's serious expression and didn't want him to look so sad. "Don't worry. We picked ourselves up and started building again," he said.

Joe pointed to a World War I SPAD fighter plane in various stages of completion. "Here's our newest project," he said. Three men were busy fitting a wing to the side of the plane. "Meet my crew, Harry, Richard, and Wild Bill!" The men smiled and waved. "With us working out in the open like this, people can come here and watch her being built, piece by piece."

"Do many people come to the Yankee Air Museum?" Mimi asked.

"Yes, thousands, actually," Joe said. "We have air shows several times a year." He tapped his chest. "I'm the docent here, so I speak to hundreds of Boy and Girl Scouts and others just interested in old war planes. We get a lot of new members that way.

"Come to think of it," Joe continued, "I have a little something you might like." He searched around on his workbench, picked up a folded T-shirt, and handed it to Grant. "Now you're an official junior member of the Yankee Air Museum! I hope you'll come back when you grow up so you can help us restore some war birds too."

Grant held up the shirt with a picture of the *Yankee Lady* bomber on the front. "Wow! Thanks, Mr. Joe!" he said.

Joe wiped his hands on a red rag and tucked it in his back pocket. "So where are you guys heading from here?" he asked.

"We're going to lunch, then on to the Motown Museum—Hitsville U.S.A.," Mimi replied.